Bulldogs

Kate Riggs

seedlings

CREATIVE EDUCATION • CREATIVE PAPERBACKS

Published by Creative Education and Creative Paperbacks
P.O. Box 227, Mankato, Minnesota 56002
Creative Education and Creative Paperbacks
are imprints of The Creative Company
www.thecreativecompany.us

Design by Ellen Huber; production by Travis Green and Chelsey Luther; art direction by Rita Marshall

Photographs by 123rf (Tatiana Katsai, Somchai Suppalertporn), Corbis (Dann Tardif/LWA), Dreamstime (Adogslifephoto, Isselee, Patryk Kosmider), Getty Images (JB Broccard), iStockphoto (ClarkandCompany, GlobalP), Shutterstock (Eric Isselee, Tatiana Katsai, Erik Lam, otsphoto, Jenny Sturm, WilleeCole Photography), SuperStock (age fotostock, Juniors, NaturePL)

Library of Congress Cataloging-in-Publication Data
Riggs, Kate.
Bulldogs / Kate Riggs.
p. cm. — (Seedlings)
Includes bibliographical references and index.
Summary: A kindergarten-level introduction to bulldogs, covering their personalities, behaviors, life span, and such defining features as their ears.
ISBN 978-1-60818-662-4 (hardcover)
ISBN 978-1-62832-247-7 (pbk)
ISBN 978-1-56660-676-9 (eBook)
1. Bulldog—Juvenile literature. 2. Dog breeds—Juvenile literature. I. Title. II. Series: Seedlings.
SF429.B85R54 2016
636.72—dc23 2015007563
CCSS: RI.K.1, 2, 3, 4, 5, 6, 7; RI.1.1, 2, 3, 4, 5, 6, 7; RF.K.1, 3; RF.1.1

TABLE OF CONTENTS

Hello, bulldogs!

Bulldogs are gentle breeds of dogs. They love to be around people.

Wide-bodied bulldogs have short noses. Their skin has wrinkles everywhere.

French bulldogs are the smallest bulldogs.

They weigh less than 30 pounds. Their ears look like a **bat**'s!

Other bulldogs are big and round.

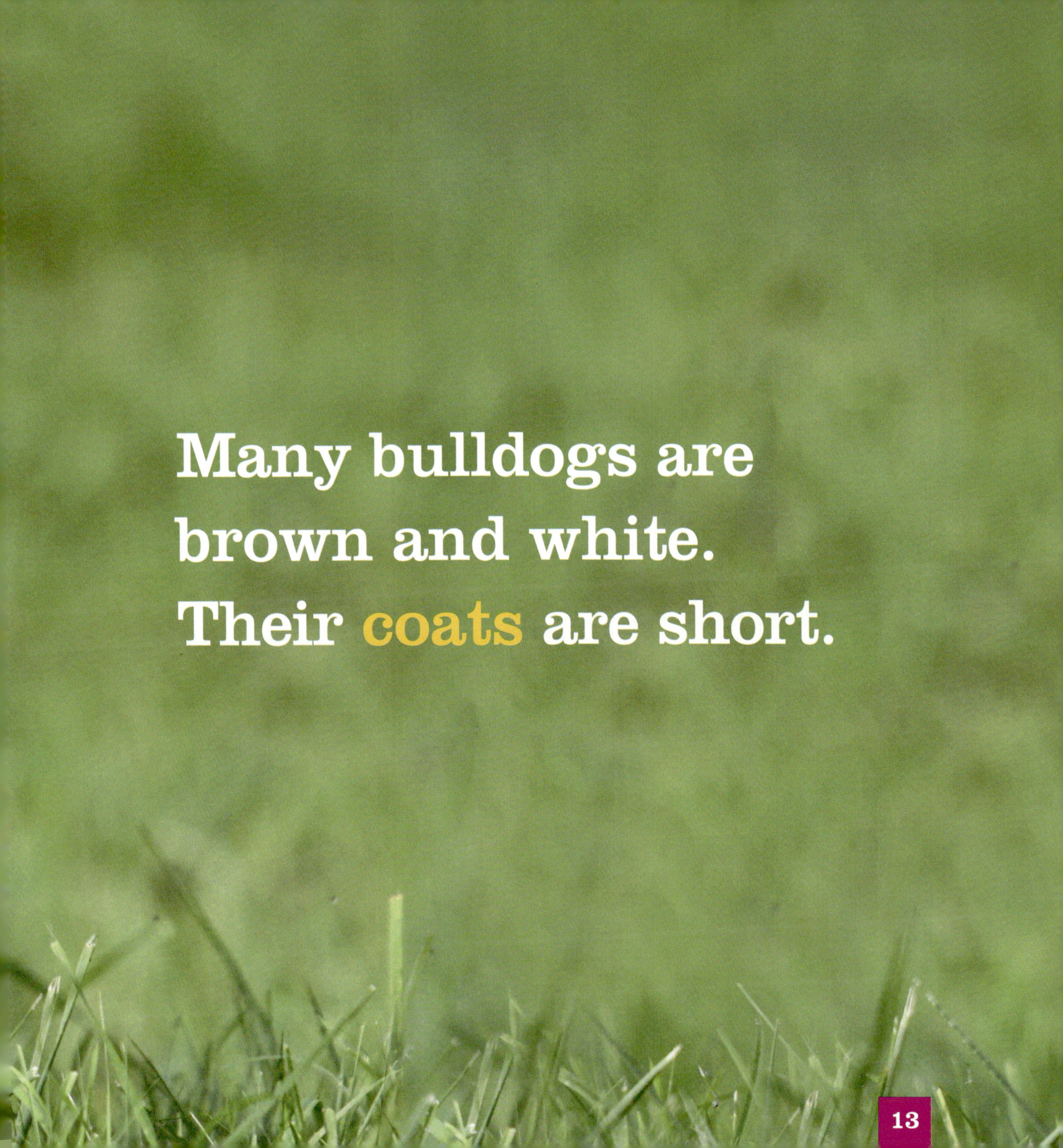

Many bulldogs are brown and white. Their **coats** are short.

A bulldog puppy runs and pounces. He makes squeaky sounds. A bulldog pet lives for about eight years.

Friendly bulldogs play and look for treats. They wag their short tails.

Goodbye, bulldogs!

Picture a Bulldog

ear
eye
nose
mouth
tooth
muzzle
claws

Words to Know

bat: an animal that flies at night and has pointed ears

breeds: groups of dogs that are alike

coats: the fur or hair of animals

Read More

Green, Sara. *Bulldogs*.
Minneapolis: Bellwether Media, 2010.

Johnson, Jinny. *Bulldog*.
Mankato, Minn.: Smart Apple Media, 2013.

Websites

Bailey's Responsible Dog Owner's Coloring Book
https://images.akc.org/pdf/public_education
/coloring_book.pdf
Print out pictures of pet dogs to color.

English Bulldog Video
http://www.animalplanet.com/tv-shows/dogs-101
/videos/english-bulldog/
Watch videos about English bulldogs and other dogs.

Index